This book belongs to...

First published in 2005
by Hodder Children's Books

This edition published in 2015

Text and illustrations copyright © Mick Inkpen 2005

Hodder Children's Books
An imprint of
Hachette Children's Group
Part of Hodder & Stoughton
Carmelite House
50 Victoria Embankment
London EC4Y 0DZ

The right of Mick Inkpen to be identified as the author
and illustrator of this Work has been asserted by him in
accordance with the Copyright, Designs and Patents Act 1988.

A catalogue record of this book is available from the British Library.

ISBN: 978 1 444 94263 7

10 9 8 7 6 5 4 3 2 1

Printed in China

An Hachette UK Company
www.hachette.co.uk

Tickly Christmas Wibbly Pig!

Mick Inkpen

Hodder
Children's
Books

An imprint of Hachette Children's Group

Wibbly Pig has a
Christmas scarf,
made last year,
especially for him,
by Big Aunt Larlie.
So it is very special.

He doesn't like it
very much.

Wibbly has
special gloves too.
One of them
arrived the
Christmas before last.

And the other arrived
the Christmas
before that.
Can you guess
who made them?

Big Aunt Larlie.

The Christmas before
all of these Christmases,
Wibbly Pig was just
a little, baby piglet.
And he looked
like this.
        And Big Aunt Larlie
    was to blame.

Wibbly's special scarf and gloves are tickly.

Itch!
Ooch!
Ouch!

But when it's cold outside, and snow has fallen, Wibbly Pig must wear his special scarf, and his special gloves. It's expected.

It is ten days before Christmas, and Wibbly Pig is helping to put up the Christmas decorations.

This year, for the very first time, Big Aunt Larlie is coming to stay.

Big Aunt Larlie has bought herself some balls of wool – more balls of wool than usual.

Click! Clack! go her knitting needles.

Something very special is on the way.

Oh no.

Wibbly's friends do not have aunties like Big Aunt Larlie.

'I wonder what I will get this year,' says Wibbly Pig. 'I have tickly gloves. I have a tickly scarf.'

'I know!' says Spotty Pig. 'A tickly hat!'

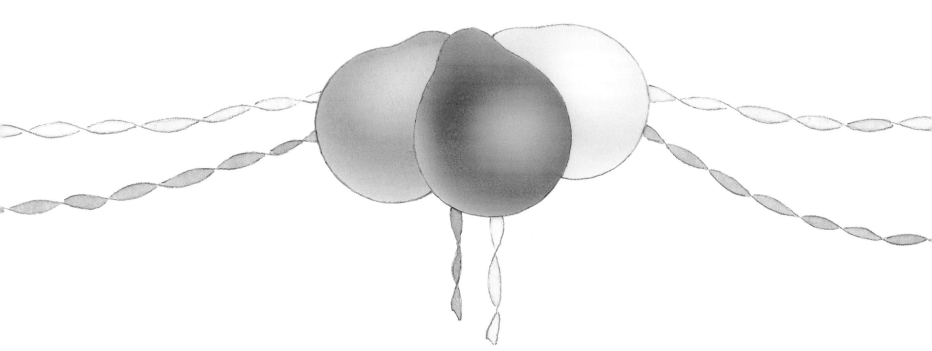

It's Christmas Eve and
Wibbly Pig is investigating
Christmas parcels.
Itch! Ooch! Ouch!
The tree is tickly too!
Just like the hat he will
get from Big Aunt Larlie.

Ding! Dong! goes the doorbell.
It's Big Aunt Larlie, come to stay.

Wibbly Pig is surprised.
'Aunt Larlie!' he says. 'You're wearing my present!'

Big Aunt Larlie laughs. 'No I'm not, Wibbly dear!' she says. 'This year I've made a special Christmas outfit for myself!

This is YOUR present!'

There is no tickly hat for Wibbly Pig! Oh dear! What a shame!

This year Wibbly Pig will have to make do with…

...whooosh!

A toboggan!

Happy Christmas, Wibbly Pig!

Great Kipper books
to share together

Kipper's
Birthday

Mick Inkpen

Mick Inkpen

Kipper

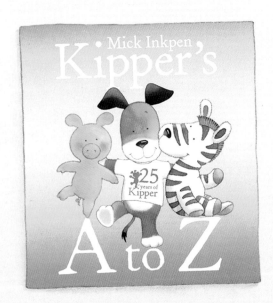

Mick Inkpen

Kipper's

A to Z

Kipper's
Christmas Eve

Mick Inkpen